DISNEY
FROZEN
TROLL MAGIC

Adapted by Cynthia Hands
Illustrated by the Disney Storybook Artists

A GOLDEN BOOK • NEW YORK

Copyright © 2013 Disney Enterprises, Inc. All rights reserved. Published in the United States by
Golden Books, an imprint of Random House Children's Books, a division of Random House, Inc., 1745 Broadway,
New York, NY 10019, and in Canada by Random House of Canada Limited, Toronto, in conjunction with Disney
Enterprises, Inc. Golden Books, A Golden Book, and the G colophon are registered trademarks of Random House, Inc.

ISBN 978-0-7364-3062-3
randomhouse.com/kids
CRAYONS MANUFACTURED IN CHINA
Book printed in the United States of America
10 9 8 7 6 5 4 3 2 1

Anna is the youngest princess in the kingdom of Arendelle.

Prince Hans is visiting Arendelle for a royal celebration.

Anna falls for Hans on their very first meeting.

Circle the picture of Anna that is different from the others.

A

B

C

D

E

Anna doesn't always get along with her older sister, Elsa.

Elsa is about to become the new queen of Arendelle!

Queen Elsa has a beautiful, sparkly crown.
Circle the crown that matches the one she is wearing.

A

B

F

C

E

D

Hans and Anna say they're in love,
but Elsa does not want them to get married.

Elsa wears gloves to hide a secret, but Anna learns the truth.

Elsa can freeze anything she touches—
and now all of Arendelle is covered with ice!

Anna asks Hans to watch over the kingdom.

Far away, Elsa creates an ice palace with her powers.

Anna wants to find Elsa and bring her back home.

Solve the maze to help Anna through the snowstorm.

Start →

→ Finish

ANSWER

Kristoff is a rugged mountain man.

Anna meets Kristoff at the trading post
and asks him to help her find Elsa.

Kristoff's reindeer, Sven, loves carrots!

Anna buys plenty of supplies for Kristoff and Sven.
How many carrots can you find in the barn?

Olaf is a little snowman with a big heart.

Anna makes a new friend!

Kristoff and Anna enjoy the sights on their way to the ice palace.

Back in Arendelle, Hans takes charge
and sets off to find Anna.

Look up, down, forward, backward, and diagonally
to find all the names.

Anna

Kristoff

H	W	G	K
A	A	B	R
N	U	N	I
N	E	V	S
A	A	M	T
J	S	D	O
O	L	A	F
C	E	Q	F

Sven

Olaf

Elsa

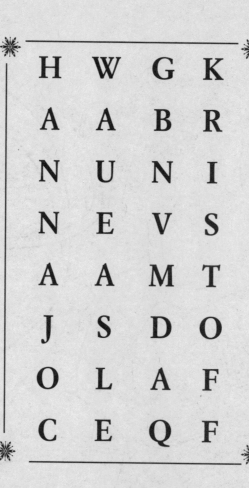

Hans

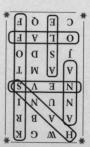

ANSWER:

Elsa reigns as the Snow Queen of her ice palace.

Anna is mad that Elsa refuses to come home.

Draw a line between each picture and its three close-ups.

Anna

Elsa

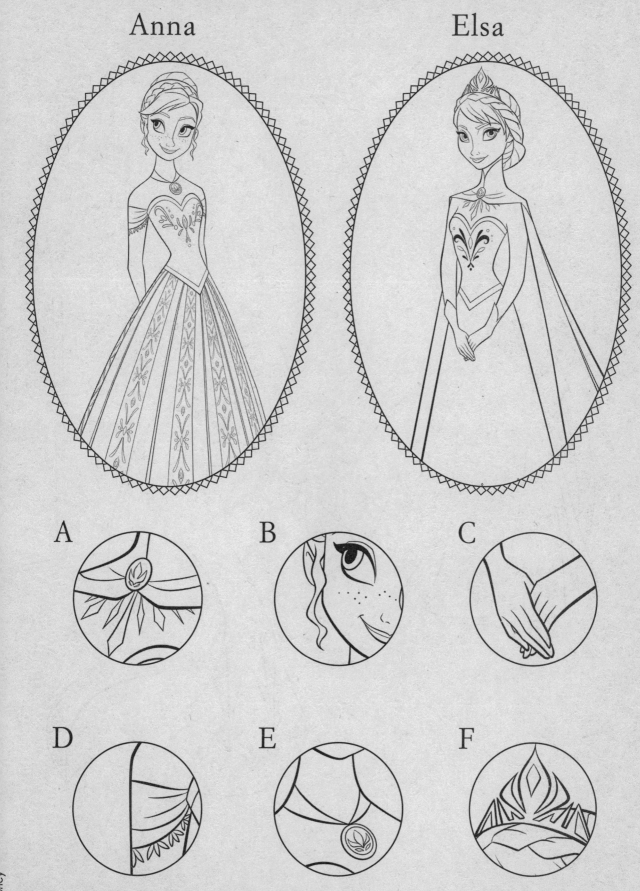

A

B

C

D

E

F

Elsa accidentally pushes Anna away with an icy blast.

Elsa did not mean to hurt her sister.

Olaf names Elsa's giant snowman.
Use the snowflake code to find out his name!

| A | H | L | M | O | R | S | W |

___ ___ ___ ___ ___ ___ ___ ___ ___ ___ ___

The giant snowman chases Kristoff and Anna
through the forest.

The icy blast from Elsa makes Anna start to freeze.

The trolls will know how to save Anna!
Can you help her find the path to the old troll?

Start

3

2

1

Finish

The old troll tells Anna that only an act of true love can save her.

Kristoff carries Anna back to Arendelle in search of help.

Anna believes that a kiss from Hans can melt her frozen heart.

Hans won't kiss Anna. He leaves her to freeze instead!

Time is running out for Anna!
How many times can you find ICE in the puzzle?
Look up, down, forward, backward, and diagonally.

```
I   I   E   E
E   C   I   C
I   E   E   I
C   I   C   E
```

Elsa never meant to hurt her sister.

Kristoff has come back. He loves Anna!

Hans tries to attack Elsa—but Anna stops him!

The power of love is stronger than ice.
After saving Elsa, Anna starts to thaw.

Elsa and Anna will never take each other for granted again.

Anna is in awe of Elsa's powers.

Elsa uses her ice power to keep Olaf from melting.
Circle the two pictures that are exactly the same.

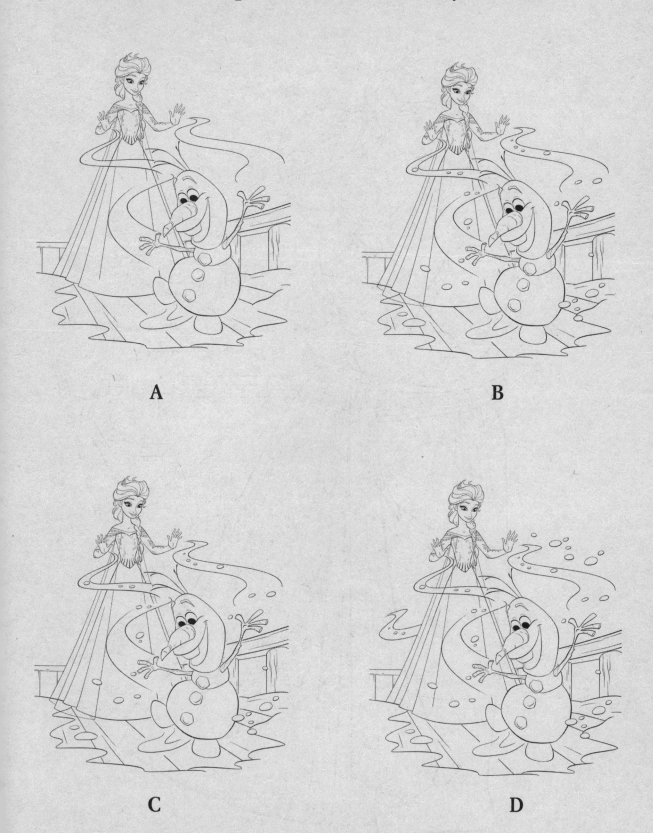

A

B

C

D

Anna and Kristoff enjoy the warmth of summer.

Anna is happy to see her friend Sven.

All is well once more in the kingdom of Arendelle.